Tom and Ricky

and the

Tree House Mystery

Bob Wright

High Noon Books
Novato, California

Cover Design and Illustrations: Herb Heidinger

Glossary: fake, mess

International Standard Book Number: 0-87879-338-0

7 6 5 4 3 2 1 0 9 8
4 3 2 1 0 9 8 7 6 5

High Noon Books
a division of ATP
20 Commercial Blvd.
Novato, California 94949

Contents

CHAPTER 1

A Good Idea

Tom got off his bike. He was in front of Ricky's house. He didn't see Ricky or Patches. But he did hear Patches barking.

"Ricky! Ricky!" Tom called.

Ricky didn't answer.

Tom called again. Ricky still didn't answer. But Tom could still hear Patches.

Ricky was in the house. He was washing Patches. Patches wanted to jump out of the tub. He could hear Tom. He wanted to see him.

"Patches! Stay still," Ricky said.

Tom called out again. This time Patches jumped out of the tub. He was all wet. He ran to the front door. Ricky ran after him.

Tom saw Patches. He could see that Patches was all wet.

"Stay down, Patches! Stay down," Tom said.

Patches didn't care. He jumped all over Tom.

"Now we're both wet," Tom said.

"I was almost done washing him," Ricky said.

"Let me help you," Tom said.

"No, I'll stop now," Ricky said.

"He's almost clean," Tom said.

"Let's dry him off," Ricky said.

"OK," Tom said.

Ricky got some old rags.

"Give me some of those. We can get this done fast," Tom said.

Patches sat still. He wanted to be dry again.

"Why did you wash him today?" Tom asked.

"He was dirty. He was very dirty. He went to the creek with me," Ricky said.

"What were you doing there?" Tom asked.

"I was going to fish. Patches jumped in the water and mud. The fish went away. Patches had mud all over him," Ricky answered.

"He's clean now," Tom said.

"Here are some more rags. Dry yourself off," Ricky said.

Tom took the rags to dry himself.

Tom and Ricky sat down. Patches was dry now and so were they.

"Now what are you going to do?" Tom asked.

"Want to make a tree house?" Ricky asked.

"A tree house?" Tom said.

"I saw a good place for a tree house down at the creek," Ricky said.

"Is it a big tree?" Tom asked.

"It sure is," Ricky answered.

"Is it near the creek?" Tom asked.

"Right by the creek," Ricky answered.

"We could fish in the creek. Then we could use the tree house to rest," Tom asked.

"That's what I was thinking," Ricky said.

"How long will it take to make it?" Tom asked.

"Not long. I think we could do it in one day," Ricky said.

"Well, let's do it," Tom said.

"Come on. I'll show you where the tree is," Ricky said.

They got on their bikes. Patches barked.

"OK, Patches. You can come with us. But don't run in the water again," Ricky said.

CHAPTER 2

The Dark Blue Car

The creek was near Ricky's house. It didn't take long to get there.

They went down Front Street. That was the fast way to get there.

All of a sudden a dark, old blue car went by them. It was going fast.

"Let's stay by the side of the street," Ricky called out.

"You're right. He was going fast," Tom said.

They were getting near the creek. They could see the trees over the hill.

"I can see all the trees now," Tom said.

"Keep on going. It is near here," Ricky said.

They got over the hill and down by the creek.

"There sure are a lot of trees. Which one is it?" Tom asked.

"That one," Ricky said.

They got off their bikes.

"Come on. Let me show you where we can make the tree house," Ricky said.

They walked over to the big tree.

"See. Right up there. Look. Can you see the place?" Ricky asked.

Tom looked up at the tree. He could see that they could make a good tree house in it.

Ricky looked around. "Where's Patches?"

"Oh, no! Look! He's back in the creek!" Tom answered.

"Patches! Come here!" Ricky called.

Patches didn't come. He was in the creek barking at the fish.

"Come here, Patches," Ricky called again.

This time Patches came.

"Look at him. He's all dirty again!" Ricky said.

"And he's all wet," Tom said.

Patches ran to Ricky.

"Don't get near me. Just sit," Ricky said.

Patches sat down. He didn't move.

"Well, where do we start?" Tom asked.

"We need to get some wood," Ricky said.

"Oh, no! Look! He's back in the creek!"

"Do you have any at home?" Tom asked.

"My dad has some. I think we can use it," Ricky answered.

"Will it take much wood to make it?" Tom asked.

"No, I don't think so," Ricky answered.

"How will we get up into the tree?" Tom asked.

"I have a rope ladder at home. We can use that to get up and down," Ricky said.

"OK. Let's get going," Tom said.

"Right. We have a lot to do," Ricky said.

They got on their bikes. Patches jumped up. He was dry now. And he was ready to go.

"Come on, Patches," Ricky called.

They rode their bikes up away from the creek. Then they got onto the street to ride home.

All of a sudden the dark, old blue car passed them. It was going fast.

"Did you see that?" Ricky called to Tom.

"I sure did! They almost hit me!" Tom called back.

"Isn't that the same car we saw when we came here?" Tom asked.

"I think so. It sure looks the same," Ricky answered.

"Well, let's get back home," Tom said.

"Right," Ricky called back.

CHAPTER 3

Lots of Wood

Ricky's dad was working on the car. He saw Tom and Ricky with Patches running in back of them.

"Dad," Ricky called out.

"I'm over here. What's up?" he said.

"We're going to make a tree house," Ricky said.

"A tree house? Where?" his dad asked.

"Down by the creek," Ricky answered.

"We found a good tree. It will be a good place for the tree house," Tom said.

"Is the tree near the creek?" Ricky's dad asked.

"It sure is," Ricky answered.

"We can fish. Then we can rest in the tree house," Tom said.

"We might want to sleep there when it is done," Ricky said.

"I made a tree house when I was a kid. How can I help?" Ricky's dad asked.

"We need some wood. Can we take some from here?" Ricky asked.

"Let me see what I have. I'm going to use some of it," he answered.

Ricky's dad went over to the wood pile. He looked at all the wood.

"You will have to cut some of this wood. It might be too long the way it is."

"That's OK. We can cut it here. Then we will put it on our bikes," Ricky said.

"Well, let's see. It might take a long time to get all of the wood there. I might be done with the car by that time," his dad said.

"Where's the saw?" Tom asked.

"Here. Use this one," Ricky's dad said. He gave them his good saw.

Tom and Ricky worked together. It didn't take long to saw all the wood.

They stood and looked at all the wood.

"I knew there would be a lot," Ricky's dad said.

"It will take a long time to get all the wood to the creek," Ricky said.

"Our bikes won't hold it all," Tom said.

Tom and Ricky worked together.

"Well, I'm done with the car. Let's put all the wood in it. I'll take it over to the creek. You can go on your bikes. We'll meet there," Ricky's dad said.

They all got the wood in the car. Patches jumped in with Ricky's dad.

"What about the rope ladder?" Tom asked.

"That's right. I forgot about it. I'll get it," Ricky said.

"What are you going to do with that?" Ricky's dad asked.

"We're going to use it to get up and down the tree," Tom said.

"OK. I'll meet you there," Ricky's dad said.

CHAPTER 4

Making the Tree House

Tom and Ricky got to the creek first. They looked around for Ricky's dad.

"I don't see your dad," Tom said.

"He should have been here first," Ricky said.

"Look. There he is. I see him. He's up by the street," Ricky said.

Ricky's dad got out of the car. He walked down to the creek with Patches.

"Why are you so late?" Ricky asked.

"I almost got hit by an old car," he answered.

"An old blue car?" Tom said.

"Do you know that car?" Ricky's dad asked.

"We sure do. It almost hit us two times today," Ricky said.

"I tried to go after it, but it got away. That's why I'm late," he said.

"I think they are going to hurt someone," Tom said.

"I hope it isn't us," Ricky said.

"They must be far away by now. Well, where do we put the wood?" Ricky's dad asked.

"We can take it out of the car. We'll put it right here," Ricky said.

"First, show me the tree you are going to use," Ricky's dad said.

"There it is. That one," Tom said.

Ricky's dad walked around the tree. He didn't say anything. Then he looked over at the creek.

"I like it. It is near the creek. It looks safe to me," he said.

"We think so, too," Ricky answered.

"OK. Let's get that wood," Tom said.

They all went back to the car. Each one got a load of wood. They had to go back to the car many times.

"Well, that's it," Ricky's dad said.

"We have all the wood here," Ricky said.

"I'll be going. Don't stay too late," Ricky's dad said.

"What about Patches? He'll be in the way if he stays with us," Tom said.

"I'll take him with me. Come on, Patches. You're going home with me," Ricky's dad said.

Patches barked and ran to the car.

"I hope you don't see that blue car again," Ricky called out.

"Me, too," his dad answered and left.

"We'll see you later," Tom called.

"Let's get to work. We have a lot to do," Ricky said.

"I'll get up into the tree," Tom said.

"And I'll hand you the wood," Ricky said.

Little by little Ricky got the wood up to Tom. They used the rope ladder to help pull the wood up.

Little by little Ricky got the wood up to Tom.

Tom worked up in the tree.

"Let me get up there now," Ricky said.

"OK. I'll get down and hand you the wood," Tom said.

They got the walls done. Then Tom said, "It looks good, doesn't it?"

"It sure does," Ricky said.

"Let's sleep here tonight," Tom said.

"OK. We'll have to go home for our sleeping bags and sleep overnight," Ricky said.

They got out of the tree.

"Fix the rope ladder so no one will see it," Ricky said.

"This will be fun," Tom said.

"It sure will," Ricky answered.

CHAPTER 5

The Man and Woman

Tom and Ricky got back to the house. Then Ricky talked to his dad.

"Dad, we want to sleep in the tree house tonight. Is it OK?" Ricky asked.

"Is it safe?" his dad asked.

"The tree house will hold both of us," Tom said.

"And no one goes to the creek at night," Ricky said.

"I think it will be OK," Ricky's dad said.

"Tom, call your dad. Make sure it is all right with him," Ricky said.

Tom called his dad.

"He said I can sleep over," Tom said.

Tom and Ricky got their sleeping bags.

"Take your coats," Ricky's mother said.

Patches looked at them.

"OK, Patches. You can come along, too," Ricky said.

"Take care. See you in the morning," Ricky's dad said.

They got on their bikes. Patches was in back of them. They had their fishing poles with them.

It was getting dark. They went down Front Street.

"Look, Tom. There's that car again," Ricky called out.

Tom stopped his bike. So did Ricky.

The blue car went by them very fast.

"Who are they? They are going to hit some-one," Ricky said.

The car did not stop. It kept going.

Tom and Ricky got to the creek. It was so dark it was hard to find the tree.

"There it is. I know that's it. It's near the creek. That's how I know it," Ricky said.

They got the rope ladder down.

"You go up. I'll stay here with Patches," Ricky said.

Tom took his sleeping bag with him.

Then he came back down. "I'll take your sleeping bag up. Then you can bring Patches up," Tom said to Ricky.

"We can leave the fishing poles here," Ricky said.

Tom took Ricky's sleeping bag up into the tree house.

"OK, Ricky. Come on up," Tom called down.

Ricky picked up Patches. He grabbed on to the rope ladder and went up. Patches didn't bark. He didn't do anything.

Ricky put Patches inside the tree house. Patches sat in a corner and didn't move.

Tom and Ricky opened their sleeping bags.

It was very dark now. And it was cold.

"I think we can fish in the morning," Tom said.

"We'll get up early," Ricky said.

Both of them got into their sleeping bags.

"It sure is quiet out here," Tom said.

"It sure is. I don't hear anything," Ricky said.

All of a sudden Patches barked.

"Patches, be quiet," Ricky said.

"Wait, Ricky. I think I hear something," Tom said.

"What is it?" Ricky asked.

"I can hear someone talking," Tom said.

"There isn't anyone near here," Ricky said.

"I know I heard someone talking," Tom said.

Tom and Ricky didn't say anything. Ricky wanted to see if he could hear anything.

"I hear it, too. It is a man. He must be near here," Ricky said.

"Ricky, he must be near the tree," Tom said.

They could hear the man talking now. "This is the place. We can hide the things here. No one will see this place. What do you think?"

Then they heard a woman. "I like it. It's a good place. We can come back in the morning," a woman said.

"OK. Let's go back to the car," the man said.

Ricky looked out from the tree house.

"I see them going away. They are going up to Front Street. That's where they must have their car," Ricky said.

"What do they mean about putting things here?" Tom asked.

"I'd sure like to know," Ricky said.

CHAPTER 6

Lots of Boxes

The sun came out early in the morning. Tom woke up first. Then Patches jumped up. He wanted to get out of the tree house. Then Ricky woke up.

"Come on, Tom. Let's go fishing," Ricky said.

They got up and rolled up their sleeping bags.

"We can leave them here," Ricky said.

"OK with me," Tom said.

Tom went down the rope ladder. Then Ricky came down with Patches.

"Where are the fishing poles?" Tom asked.

"I left them right here by the tree," Ricky said.

"I bet they took our poles," Tom said.

"I bet they did, too," Ricky said.

"Well, we can't fish now," Tom said.

"Let's get our bikes," Ricky said.

"It was good that we hid them in the bushes," Tom said.

"That was a good idea. Maybe they would have taken our bikes, too," Ricky said.

"Come on. We'll go back home," Tom said.

"They got on their bikes and went up onto Front Street.

"Ricky, there's that dark blue car again. It's going fast," Tom said.

"What's going on? Why do we keep on seeing that car?" Ricky asked.

"I wish I knew who they are," Tom said.

"Me, too. I'd tell them not to go so fast," Ricky said.

They started back for Ricky's house.

Ricky's dad saw them coming. "How did it go?" he called to them.

Tom and Ricky told him about hearing the man and woman in the dark. They told him about seeing the dark blue car again.

"I want to go back there with you. I don't like all of this," Ricky's dad said.

"Tom and I will go back again today. We'll see if anyone has been in the tree house," Ricky said.

"That will be fine. Right now, I need you to help me," Ricky's dad said.

Tom left. Ricky went to help his dad.

Tom was back at Ricky's house at 3:00.

"Come on, Ricky. Let's get back to the tree house," Tom said.

"Dad, we're going back to the tree house. We won't stay there very long," Ricky said.

They went as fast as they could back to the creek and the tree house.

Ricky got the rope ladder and went up the tree. Then Tom went up.

"Tom, look. It's full of things," Ricky said.

"Tom, look. It's full of things," Ricky said.

"It all looks new to me," Tom said.

There were coats, hats, and shoes.

"What's going on? Ricky said.

"Someone found the tree house. Someone is using it to hide things," Tom said.

"What are we going to do? I don't want to stay here," Ricky said.

"Come on. Let's go," Tom said.

They got on their bikes. They went up to Front Street. The blue car was there.

Tom and Ricky rode by the car and looked in it.

"Did you see what I saw?" Ricky called.

"I sure did. That car is full of boxes," Tom said.

"The boxes in that car look like the ones we saw in the tree house. I think that man and woman are using the tree house. I think they are taking things. Then they put them there. They are hiding things in our tree house," Ricky said.

"Let's get back to your house and tell your dad what's going on," Tom said.

CHAPTER 7

Sergeant Collins Helps

"Dad! Dad!" Ricky called.

"Here I am. What is it?" his dad said.

Ricky told him about the tree house and the things in it. They told him about seeing the blue car all filled with boxes.

"I think you should call Sergeant Collins. That man and woman may be taking those things from stores. I think they are using your tree house to hide them. They may think no one knows about the tree house," his dad said.

"Dad, will you call Sergeant Collins? Tom and I should get back to the tree house. We might see them again. We can meet you there," Ricky said.

"OK. You two get going," his dad answered.

Tom and Ricky got back on their bikes. They saw the blue car parked near the creek. They hid their bikes in the bushes.

"The car is here. But I don't see that man and woman," Tom said.

"I bet they are back at the tree house. Come on. Let's go over there. But don't let them see us," Ricky said.

They hid in the bushes near the creek.

"There they are," Tom said.

"I can hear them now," Ricky said.

"Get everything out of the tree house," the man said.

"What about those boys we keep on seeing?" the woman said.

"They have been around here a lot. They might find our hiding place," the man said.

The woman used the rope ladder to get up into the tree house.

"I need some help. I can't do this all by myself," she said.

"OK, OK, I'll help you," he said.

The woman looked out from the tree house.

"There are a lot of boxes up here. Come on up and help me," she called out.

"OK! OK! I'll be right up there," he called back.

The man went up the rope ladder.

All of a sudden the woman looked out from the tree house and called, "Look! Look! I see those two boys. They are over there in the bushes."

"Where?" the man said.

"Right over there," she said.

Tom looked out from the bushes. "They see us. What do we do now?" he asked.

"Get the rope ladder! Pull it down," Ricky said.

They ran over to the tree. Ricky pulled the ladder down.

"Now what do we do?" the woman asked.

"Jump! Let's jump!" he said.

"No way. I'm not jumping," she said.

"Look! Look! I see those two boys."

"Well, I'm going to," he said. The man jumped from the tree house down to the ground.

"Come on! Let's get him," Ricky called.

The man started to yell. "Stop! Stop! I'm hurt. Help me. I'm hurt!"

Tom and Ricky ran over to him. He was rolling all over the ground. He couldn't get up.

Just then Ricky saw his dad and Sergeant Collins.

"Boy, are we glad to see you!" Tom said.

"We saw the man jump," Sergeant Collins said.

"What about the woman?" Ricky's dad said.

"I'll see that she gets down. Help me get the rope ladder, Tom," Sergeant Collins said.

Tom helped Sergeant Collins get the rope ladder back up into the tree. "OK. You can come down now," Sergeant Collins called out to the woman.

The woman was mad. She was yelling at the man. "I told you not to use that tree house. We never should have used it."

"Don't say anything," the man called back to her.

"OK, you two. I'm taking you in. I have my car up on Front Street," Sergeant Collins said.

"But I can't walk," the man said.

"I'll help you. Come on," Sergeant Collins said.

The Sergeant pulled the man up.

"It sure was a close call," Tom said.

"What about all those things in the tree house?" Ricky asked.

"The police will take care of those things," Ricky's dad said.

"Let's all go back home," Tom said.

"We have to get our sleeping bags," Ricky said.

They went back up into the tree house.

"I bet we can sleep here again," Ricky said.

"Do you think we can?" Tom asked.

"I know we can," Ricky answered.

"But next time we'll hide our fishing poles!" Tom said.